BABAR
Isabelle the Flower Girl

Harry N. Abrams, Inc., Publishers

Isabelle was very excited. She had been asked to be the flower girl at a wedding!

"What will I have to do?" she asked her mother.

"Well," said Celeste, "most likely, you'll carry a basket of rose petals and sprinkle them around. You also might hold trunks with the boy who is the ring-bearer."

"Hold trunks with a boy!" said Isabelle. "Ewww!"
Celeste just smiled.

There was plenty of time to get ready before the wedding. Isabelle was still excited, but now it seemed there were many things to worry about.

First she tried on her dress.

"It's very pretty!" said Celeste.

"I don't know," said Isabelle. "I think the sleeves are yucky."

Then came the shoes.

"Those are nice!" said Flora.

"I'm afraid they'll pinch while I'm walking down the aisle," said Isabelle.

Then Isabelle started to worry about sprinkling the rose petals. What if she sprinkled too much, or too little, or in the wrong places?

But the thing Isabelle worried about most was tripping. What if she tripped, and fell, and dropped her basket of rose petals right in front of everyone?

It was too awful to think about. But she did think about it, a lot.

At last, the big day arrived. When it was time,
Isabelle started walking down the aisle in front of the
bride, and all the guests oohed and aahed at how pretty
she was.

Isabelle walked very, very carefully—not too fast, and not too slow. She concentrated so hard, she forgot to sprinkle her rose petals!

And then, the worst possible thing happened!
Isabelle's shoe caught on the carpet, and she tripped.
She did not fall, but she stumbled just enough to send
her rose petals flying high into the air.

Isabelle felt awful. There was nothing she could do but watch as the rose petals gently fell all around, almost like snow.

The petals fell softly onto the ringbearer's pillow.
They fell on the bridesmaids.
They fell on the groom, and they fell on the bride.

"Oooh," sighed everyone. "How beautiful!"
When she heard that, Isabelle knew it would all
be okay.

The bride and the groom exchanged vows. Isabelle did not understand all the words they said, but she knew they were important.

After the ceremony ended, everyone ate, sang,
danced, and had a good time.

The bride took Isabelle aside. "You were a wonderful flower girl," she said. "Did you have fun?"
"Yes," said Isabelle. "I really did!"

Design by Vivian Cheng
Production Manager: Jonathan Lopes

Library of Congress Cataloging-in-Publication Data

Isabelle the flower girl /
p. cm.
"Babar"—T.p.
Summary: When Isabelle agrees to be a flower girl at a wedding, she is so concerned about doing some-
thing wrong that she almost forgets to have fun.
ISBN 0-8109-5039-1 (alk. paper)
[1. Weddings—Fiction. 2. Elephants—Fiction. 3. Kings, queens, rulers, etc.] I. Brunhoff, Jean de,
1899–1937. II. Brunhoff, Laurent de, 1925– III. Title.

PZ7.W44715Is 2004
[E]—dc22
2004002454

Printed and bound in China
10 9 8 7 6 5 4 3 2 1

Harry N. Abrams, Inc.
100 Fifth Avenue
New York, NY 10011
www.abramsbooks.com

Abrams is a subsidiary of LA MARTINIÈRE GROUPE